ORANGUTAN

illustrated by Lynne Cherry

E. P. DUTTON • NEW YORK

Orangutans live
in the thick green rain forest...

where they
swing…swing…
slowly through the treetops.

Wherever mother orangutan goes,
baby goes too.
Orangutans take good care
of their little ones.

Young orangutans play alone

or together.

It's raining in the forest. The orangutans are dry inside their nest.

for Julie Lee,
my good friend and fellow lover of for

Text copyright © 1987 by E. P. Dutton
Illustrations copyright © 1987 by Lynne Cherry

All rights reserved.
Licensed by World Wildlife Fund®

Published in the United States by E. P. Dutton,
2 Park Avenue, New York, N.Y. 10016

Published simultaneously in Canada by
Fitzhenry & Whiteside Limited, Toronto

Text and editing: Lucia Monfried   Designer: Isabel Warren-Lynch

Printed in Singapore by Tien Wah Press
First Edition   CUSA & P   10 9 8 7 6 5 4 3 2 1

Library of Congress Cataloging-in-Publication Data

Cherry, Lynne.
  Orangutan.

  (Help save us books)
  Summary: A look at orangutans in the rain forest as
they swing through the treetops and care for their babies.
  1. Orangutan—Pictorial works—Juvenile literature.
[1. Orangutan] I. Monfried, Lucia. II. Title.
III. Series.
QL737.P96C47 1987   599.88'42   86-24025
ISBN 0-525-44301-0